STEVE HARTLEY

DANNY BAKER RECORD BREAKER

THE WORLD'S
LOUDEST ARMPIT FART

ILLUSTRATED BY KATE PANKHURST

MACMILLAN CHILDREN'S BOOKS

First published 2010 by Macmillan Children's Books
a division of Macmillan Publishers Limited
20 New Wharf Road, London N1 9RR
Basingstoke and Oxford
Associated companies throughout the world
www.panmacmillan.com

ISBN 978-0-330-50918-3

1 3 5 7 9 8 6 4 2

A CIP catalogue record for this book is available from
the British Library.

Printed and bound in the UK by CPI Mackays Chatham ME5 8TD

For Rosie

This is entirely a work of fiction and any resemblance
to the real world is purely coincidental.

The Wibbly
Wobbly Wonder

WARNING! SHE'S BACK!

THE PENLEYDALE CLARION

Dirty Do-ings in Burly Bottoms!

By Reginald Heap, Chief News Reporter

An illegal Yorkshire cheese caused uproar last weekend at the finish of the Penleydale Junior Uphill Cheese-rolling Race.

For the 143rd year running, competitors pushed their regulation circular thirty centimetre Waxy Penleydale Cheeses along the traditional ten-kilometre course. The route took them up Boggart's Nose, across Miggin's Mop and over Hangman's Hump, before finally dropping down into Burly Bottoms.

With the finishing line in sight, the temperature hit a Penleydale record of 33.7°C. The lead cheese, being rolled by new-boy Maradona

'The Cheeseboy' Potts, disintegrated and melted, and roller after roller was sent tumbling on the greasy liquid cheese.

Ollie 'The Drainpipe' Snodgrass, age 11, of Hogton, kept his head – and his feet – and rolled his cheese over the pile of fallen competitors to win. Local boy Danny 'Record Breaker' Baker, who won last year's race in record time, broke a small bone in his foot, but hobbled on to finish in seventh place.

Judge Harry Clegg explained, 'The Waxy Penleydale is highly resistant to extreme temperatures, and would never melt like Maradona's cheese did. Closer inspection of the offending fromage confirmed that it was an illegal Grimsdyke Crumbly, disguised to look like a Waxy Penleydale. The Grimsdyke is lighter than the Penleydale, so it's easier to push uphill.'

Maradona Potts, now renamed 'The Cheatboy', was disqualified, and banned from competing in the race For Ever (+ ten years).

Result:

1st: Ollie 'The Drainpipe' Snodgrass

2nd: Trixibelle 'Bossyboots' Wolstenholme

3rd: Kristian 'The Bookworm' Renshaw

4th: Jack 'The Teabag' Spratt

5th: Samantha 'Tufty' Tompkins

6th: Matthew 'The Calculator' Mason

7th: Danny 'Record Breaker' Baker

8th: Ryan 'The Zombie' Wilkins

9th: Steve 'Snotbucket' Snitterton

10th: Carly 'Jam Butty' Benson

Retired hurt: Tommy 'Spiffy' Spofforth, Lucy 'Nose-picker' Knowles, Billy 'The Big Toe' Bowling

Disqualified: Maradona 'The Cheatboy' Potts

Hard Cheese

To the Keeper of the Records
The Great Big Book of World Records
London

Dear Mr Bibby

I've got a plaster cast up to my knee because
I hurt my foot when I slipped on a cheese. I'm
going to miss the start of the new football
season, and my doctor said I'll be out for four
weeks. My Grandad Nobby says I'm lucky it's only
four weeks. When he slipped on the
Rotting Chowhabunga seed-pod, he was
out for four decades!

my leg

The doctor counted all the times
I've needed treatment because of my record
attempts, including:

My unwashed 207-spot bottom

My dangerously stinky feet

My walking-backwards-Wonderfluff-
   nappy-box-on-the-head incident

My boffin-baffling gobbledegook

My hospital-food-fuelled mighty trump

And my whistling, budgie-costumed, up-a-tree
   Spanish cramp.

spotty
bum

When the doctor added these to all the
other times I've been with coughs, injections,
infections and stuff, I've had to see a doctor
seventy-nine times. She said that must be a
record. I *think* she was probably joking with me,
but *is* it a record?

Best wishes

Danny Baker

PS I only need to get through one more match
without anyone scoring against me, to break
the record for Most Consecutive Games without
Conceding a Goal. Keep your fingers crossed!

7

Dear Danny

Yes, I'm afraid the doctor *was* joking with you.
The record for Highest Number of Separate
Incidents Requiring Medical Treatment belongs
to Elmer Boggs of Picatinny, New Jersey, USA.

During his lifetime, Elmer broke every bone
in his body at least once, *including* the small
bones in both ears. He pulled every muscle, and
tore every tendon. Elmer was stung by jellyfish,
bees, wasps and a scorpion, and was bitten by
185 different kinds of animal, including a cow,
a squirrel, a bushbaby, a shark, a tortoise and
a ladybird. He also had 2,469 separate diseases
and made a total of 23,423 visits to the doctor.

Unwisely for someone who had such an accident-prone life, in 1984 Elmer volunteered to put his head in a lion's mouth to raise money for charity. This, of course, was a big mistake, and when the lion sneezed . . .

Recordologists cannot agree if his death should be included in the total, as he was seen by a doctor to pronounce him dead. I think it should, so I have.

Good luck with your first game back, Danny. I hope you manage to keep a clean sheet and break another record. I'll be keeping my fingers, toes, ears, legs *and* eyes crossed!

Best wishes
Eric Bibby
Keeper of the Records

Danny and his best friend, Matthew Mason, arrived at Walchester United for the first home game of the new season. The ground was full to bursting. The crowd had been waiting all summer for this, and excitement fizzed around the stands. Danny manoeuvred his plaster cast with some difficulty along the row of seats and sat down next to Matthew. The boys joined in the singing and chanting:

'Walchester United are the best team in the world!
After Barcelona, Real Madrid, AC Milan, Juventus,
*   Man United and Chelsea!*
Oh, and Bayern Munich, Ajax and all the teams in
*   Brazil!*
And Accrington Stanley, who beat us in the Cup
*   two years ago!*
Apart from that we're the best team in the world!'

The shrill blare of trumpets echoed through the stadium and the singing turned into a mighty roar. Danny and Matthew looked towards the tunnel, just below where they sat, and saw two men scurry on to the pitch carrying a large circular sign emblazoned with the words, 'Wibberley Wobberley – the Jellies from Mobberley'.

Suddenly a huge red jelly burst through the sign and wibbled and wobbled out to the centre circle, kicking a football and waving to the crowd.

'Let's give a big Walchester United welcome to our new sponsors, Wibberley Wobberley Jellies,' announced a voice over the loud speaker. 'And say "Hello" to our new mascot, Wibbles the Dribbling Jelly!'

Wibbles wore a red peaked cap, and the see-through red plastic jelly costume ballooned out from around his neck like a horrible bell-shaped dress. His red hands stuck out from the side and his skinny red legs from the bottom.

'I don't believe it,' groaned Danny.

'It's worse than Wally the Wall!' said Matthew.

'It's even worse than Gogo La Gamba, Real Marisco's pink prawn mascot. It doesn't even look like a jelly and you can see the man inside.'

Matthew peered closer. 'Isn't that Jack Dawkins's big brother? I thought he was training to be an astronaut.'

'Looks like he became a jelly instead!'

Just then another sound cut through the cheers of the crowd.

'Daaaaaaaannnnnnnnyyyyyyyyyyyyyyyyyyy!'

The boys stared at each other in disbelief.

'It's not . . .'

'It *can't* be . . .'

'Hiiiiiiiiiyyyyyyyyyyyyyyyyaaaaaaaaaaaaaaaa!'

'It is!'

Five rows behind them, wearing a red Walchester United shirt, her bright-red hair twisted into two long pigtails and tied on the ends with ruby-red ribbons, was Sally Butterworth.

Danny cringed as he remembered his and Matthew's first meeting with Sally, in Spain just a few months before. Not only had she scored a goal against him in a game of beach-football, she had tricked him into winning his most embarrassing record of all: 18 minutes and 47 seconds of Budgie-costumed Perched-in-a-tree Kissing! Even worse, she had made him fall out with Matthew.

Sally waved furiously, then rolled her tongue and squinted. She edged along the row of seats and skipped down the stand towards them. Danny realized with horror that there was an empty seat beside him.

'Hiya!' beamed Sally. 'Remember me?'

'No, who are you?' replied Matthew.

Sally laughed, but her smile instantly turned to a look of concern as she noticed Danny's leg. 'What have you done?' she asked, sitting down in the vacant seat.

'Slipped on a cheese,' explained Danny.

'Is it broken?'

'What, my foot or the cheese?'

Sally punched Danny playfully, but hard, on the arm.

'Ow!' he complained. 'What're *you* doing here, Sally?'

'I'm with Wibberley Wobberley,' she said. 'My dad's the Regional Manager, so you'll be seeing a lot more of me from now on.'

'Your dad's a jelly salesman?' asked Matthew.

'Yeah! How cool is that?' Sally smiled at Danny and rested her hand on his. 'Do you like jelly, Danny?'

'Yeah . . .'

'I can get you as much jelly as you can eat.'

Suddenly Danny had an idea. He pulled his hand away and folded his arms.

'Could you get me enough jelly to break a record?' he asked.

'Course I can. Dad's got thousands of boxes full of "experimental" jelly-mixes that nobody wants.'

'*Experimental* jelly-mixes?'

Sally counted the different flavours on her fingers. 'Caviar and Custard.'

'Gross!'

'Turnip and Trifle.'

'Mega-gross!'

'Fig and Fish Finger.'

'Giga-gross!' said
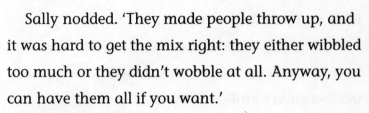
Matthew.

Sally nodded. 'They made people throw up, and it was hard to get the mix right: they either wibbled too much or they didn't wobble at all. Anyway, you can have them all if you want.'

'Ace!' said Danny.

Matthew said nothing.

'*I* broke the County Junior Jelly-juggling record, with three balls of Pepperoni Pizza and Pomegranate jelly,' boasted Sally. 'Two minutes, fifteen point four seconds.'

Danny was impressed. 'You can juggle jellies?'

'Duh! If I couldn't juggle jellies, I wouldn't have broken the County Jelly-juggling record, would I?'

Matthew nudged Danny on the arm. 'Here come the teams.'

The trumpets blared once more and the Walchester United and Downmouth Albion players ran out on to the pitch in two long lines. The roar of the crowd wrapped around Danny, Matthew and Sally and pulled them to their feet to cheer.

'By the way,' shouted Sally as the players' names were announced. 'Have you seen who your school team is playing this season?'

'No,' replied Danny. 'Why?'

Sally didn't answer. She flashed Danny a huge smile, then turned back to watch the game.

'COME ON THE WIBBERLEY WOBBERLIES!' she screamed.

The Cheatboy

Danny was looking forward to getting back to school. He hobbled on his crutches alongside Matthew as they passed through the school gates, the plaster cast on his leg now black and blue and green and red and purple and orange and pink with signatures. The name in pink was Sally Butterworth.

'I've got a record-breaking itchy leg underneath all this plaster,' he said. 'I can't wait for them to cut the cast off tomorrow.'

'I'll count the signatures at home-time and you can write to Mr Bibby at the Great Big Book of World Records to ask if it's a record.'

Danny shook his head. 'There's nowhere near enough. He'd say: "Good try, Danny! You're not going to believe this, but Thelma McCurdie's massive record-breaking 622-centimetre bottom has foiled another one of your record attempts! In January 1994, Thelma slipped on a chilli-cheese French fry and broke her bum!"'

'Mr Bibby would *never* use the word "bum",' said Matthew.

'True,' Danny grinned. 'How much plaster do you think you'd need to cover a bottom as big as that?'

Matthew shrugged. 'About three tonnes, I bet.'

'"When the cast was sawn off four months later,"' continued Danny, pretending to be Mr Bibby again. '"Officers from the Great Big Book of World Records took eleven years, five months and nineteen days to add up all the names."'

'"It took so long, because after five years, three months and twenty-nine days, they lost count and had to start again!"' laughed Matthew. '"They eventually counted twelve quidtrillion, nineteen zigzillion, six googillion, four thousand, five hundred and forty-three signatures!"'

Danny chuckled. Then he nudged his friend. 'Look, Matt!'

Mr Collinson, the Coalclough Sparrows football coach, was pinning the new season's fixture list to the school noticeboard. The boys hurried over to see who they would be playing.

'The first game's against Parpington Aardvarks,' said Matthew. 'We beat them five–nil last year. They couldn't score against you in a megatrinzillion games! You'd have broken the clean-sheet record against *them*!'

Danny didn't answer. He was looking at the team third on the list: Bunbury Bantams.

'Oh no!' he said. 'That's *her* team. We'll be playing against Sally Butterworth, and she's already scored against me.'

'That was beach football,' argued Matthew. 'It doesn't count. And anyway, you won't be fit in time for that game.'

'No, but I *will* be fit for the Junior Schools' Invitation Soccer Tournament two weeks later, and we're playing against Bunbury Bantams again!'

Just then a new kid swaggered up to them.

Danny turned and came face to face with Maradona Potts, the boy whose cheating cheese had put him in plaster.

'You!' exclaimed Danny.

'Me!' retorted Potts.

Danny lifted his plaster-covered leg. 'You did this!'

Maradona glanced down. 'Tough,' he snorted.

'What kind of a name's *Maradona*?' asked Matthew.

'My dad wanted me to be the greatest striker in the world ever. But I'm going to be the greatest goalkeeper in the world ever instead.'

'My dad's the Greatest Goalkeeper in the World Ever,' said Danny.

'Who's your dad?'

'Bobby Baker.'

'Never heard of him.'

Danny glared at the new kid. 'And *I'm* the goalie for Coalclough Sparrows.'

Maradona raised his eyebrows and stared at Danny's crutches.

'I'll be back in a couple of weeks,' said Danny.

'Tough. I'm in the team now, so you won't get your place back.'

Before Danny could reply, Potts swaggered away. 'Get used to being in the reserves, Baker,' he shouted over his shoulder. 'You're going to be there for a long time.'

'Twit,' said Danny.

'Twerp,' agreed Matthew.

The Jelly Fairy

Dear Mr Bibby

I'm in trouble with my sister, Natalie, again. It was all her fault though. Probably.

This morning, I tried to break the world record for the Tallest Free-standing Tower of Animal-shaped Jellies. I used my Auntie Sarah's wombat-shaped jelly moulds, and Wibberley Wobberley's Sausage and Satsuma jelly. I followed the instructions, but they came out too wibbly.

sausage
and
satsuma

Matthew made a giant ruler that he stuck to the wall of my house and I built the tower on the patio in front of it. He also invented a thingummyjig with a plate on the end of an extending arm, so that I could keep piling the jellies higher and higher.

I'd got the tower as high as my bedroom window when Nats came into the garden with her best friends Kaylie and Kylie. Just as I was putting another jelly on top of the pile, she yelled, 'MUM!' – snitching on me like she always does. The noise made me jump and I nudged the tower. It swung backwards, bounced off the wall, then crashed over like a tree. Natalie, Kaylie and Kylie were standing in a line and SPLAT! the jellies got all three of them.

Kylie's allergic to sausages and straight away her face swelled up in big red blotches.

Here's a picture Matthew took of my wombat-shaped jelly tower. It was 5.29 m high when it fell. Is this a record? I hope so, because today

I've got *three* girls trying to pull my ears off.

Best wishes
Danny Baker

PS I had my plaster
cast sawn off
yesterday. Now I've
got to get fit. I want
that clean-sheet
record!

Our wombat-jelly tower!

The Great Big Book
of World Records
London

ARE YOU A RECORD
BREAKER?

Dear Danny

When will you learn? Sisters and records don't
mix, and neither do sausages and satsumas, if
you ask me!

The world record for the Tallest Free-standing
Tower of Animal-shaped Jellies is held by fifteen
Outer Mongolian jelly-worshippers. Their leader,
Jelli Belli, wanted to create a Jelly Heaven
on Earth, so the group built a stone temple on
the outskirts of Ulan Bator, and filled it with
jellies of all shapes, sizes and flavours. At the
centre was a vast trembling tower of mango-
flavoured, yak-shaped jellies, 89 m high.

On 17 October 1966 a massive thunderstorm hit
Ulan Bator, with hailstones as big as tennis

25

balls. A bolt of lightning struck the jelly
tower and liquefied it instantly. The temple
filled to the top with liquid jelly and drowned
everyone inside. When the storm was over, the
jelly cooled and solidified, leaving Jelli Belli
and his group of strange jelly-worshippers
perfectly preserved in their own Jelly Heaven.
They can still be seen to this day.

I'm afraid you missed out this time, Danny, but
keep trying; there are lots of jelly records to
go for.

Best wishes
Eric Bibby
Keeper of the Records

Danny lay awake in bed. It was late and he couldn't sleep. Natalie was having a sleepover in the room next to his, and she, Kaylie and Kylie were giggling and squealing like three little pigs. But there was another reason Danny couldn't sleep: he was waiting for the moment when they finally snuggled down in their sleeping bags.

'*Eeyoooow!*'

'*Aiyeeeek!*'

'*Yeuuukkk!*'

The moment had arrived. Danny hid under his duvet and rocked with laughter.

'Mum!' yelled Natalie. 'There's something horrible in our sleeping bags!'

'It's sick!' howled Kaylie.

'It's snot!' wailed Kylie.

'It's a cowpat!' growled Natalie.

The girls appeared in Danny's doorway and glared at him.

'*Danny!*' shouted Mum. 'What have you been up to?' She stomped upstairs and into Natalie's bedroom.

Danny tried to look innocent. 'I haven't done anything!'

Mum pushed past the girls and held out a handful of jelly. 'Then how did *this* get in their sleeping bags?'

'It must have been the Jelly Fairy.'

'Mum!' cried Natalie. 'Tell him!'

'Danny,' said Mum sternly, 'I'm telling you.'

'It's only a bit of jelly,' protested Danny. 'I thought they'd like a midnight snack. It's Boiled Egg and Banana flavour.'

'Oh no!' cried Kylie. 'I'm allergic to eggs!'

Everyone stared at her feet. Sure enough, they were swelling up nicely and turning red and blotchy. Natalie grabbed the handful of jelly from Mum and hurled it at her brother.

She missed.

The next morning, Danny escaped from the house before the girls woke up. He went with his dad to watch the Coalclough Sparrows play their second game of the season.

'Maradona Potts is good, isn't he?' said Danny.

'Pretty good,' agreed Dad.

'Do you think I'll get my place back in the team when I'm fit?'

Dad ruffled Danny's hair. 'Potts is a good shot-stopper, but his positioning isn't as good as yours.'

Maradona's father barked instructions to his son from the line nearby.

'*Get those defenders sorted!*'

'*Tell that stupid centre half to get out of your way!*'

'*That box is your territory – be master of it!*'

'*Attack those crosses!*'

'*Remember, Maradona: you're the best!*'

Dad grinned at Danny and rolled his eyes.

The referee blew his whistle for the end of the game. The Sparrows had won two–nil, and Maradona had kept his second clean sheet.

'Yessss!' cheered Mr Potts. 'That's my boy! The best goalkeeper in the world ever!'

Maradona strutted from the pitch. 'Still think you'll get back in the team?' he sneered at Danny as he passed.

'Nincompoop,' whispered Danny.

'Numpty,' agreed Dad.

Sally Versus Maradona

Dear Mr Bibby

I'm having serious jelly trouble! They wobble too much and keep spoiling my records! I tried to break the Individual Keepy-uppy Jellyball-headers record using Garlic and Gooseberry flavour, but after six headers, the jelly plopped all over my noggin! I was still picking jelly out of my nose two days later. At least I had fun flicking the pickings at Natalie – she wasn't to know it was just green jelly!

After that, I tried to break the Jelly-trampoline Backward-somersault record using Tripe and Treacle mix. What a disaster! After just two backflips, the trampoline burst like a

great big water-bomb and splattered jelly all
over me, Matthew, the garden,
and Nat's knickers on the washing
line.

Nat's
pants

I got next door's dog to eat up the stuff in the
garden, but Nat's pants were ruined. She's really
had enough of my jelly pranks and was going
to tell Mum, but I offered to clean out her
rabbit hutch for two weeks.
All the straw and lettuce and
rabbit poo gave me an idea.
If we add *that* to the mix,

rabbi
po

it might make the jelly a bit stiffer. Matthew's
also experimenting by mixing different flavours
to see if he can get it right for The Big One —
we're going for the Longest Mexican Jelly-wave
in a Stadium! Can you tell me how far the wave
would have to go to be a world-beater?

Best wishes
Danny Baker

Dear Danny

Bad luck with your latest attempts. Jelly
records are never easy and getting the mix
right is vital. But I must warn you that adding
anything to your jelly (even rabbit droppings!)
would disqualify you from any record attempt:
your jellies *must* be pure. Mixing different
flavours is allowed, however.

If you find that one batch is really bouncy,
you could try the Long-distance Jelly Foot-
springs Bouncing record. This is held by Derrick
Yorick, of Warwick, who tried to bounce from
Land's End to John o' Groats with Melon and
Meringue-flavoured jellies strapped to his
boots.

His route took him through Stratford-upon-Avon, where he stopped for a few buns at the As You Lick It Pastry Shoppe. Energized by the sugary cakes, and eager to get on with his journey, Derrick began to bounce too hard and lost control of his jelly-springs. He vaulted over the wall of Falstaff's Pork-pie Factory, through an open window and straight into the factory's giant pork-pie jelly-vat.

Alas! Poor Yorick was never seen again. Falstaff's Pork Pies were unusually tasty that week, but nothing was ever proved. Derrick never knew that he had bounded to a new Long-distance Jelly Foot-springs Bouncing world record of 416.7 km.

With regard to the Mexican Jelly-wave: no one has ever managed to get right the way round a stadium before. The longest wave rolled 288 m around Uddersfield Town's Maryfield Stadium in July 1996, but broke down on the final corner. I'm sure you'll do better, Danny!

Best wishes

Eric Bibby

Keeper of the Records

The boys were in
the bathroom at
Danny's house,
trying out a new
mixture.

'What happened
to all the Hot-dog
and Halibut jelly?' asked Matthew.

'Mum ate it all,' answered Danny.
'She spread it on toast for breakfast. Since she's
been pregnant, Mum's been eating all sorts of weird
stuff. She's having jelly with everything: jelly and
chips, jelly and spaghetti . . .'

Matthew laughed. 'Maybe if she
eats enough, she'll have a jelly-
baby!'

'Do you need Hot-dog and
Halibut for the mix?'

'No. I think I've
got *this* mix just
right.' Matthew
poked the jelly with

his finger. It trembled frantically for a few seconds and then was still.

'Ace!' said Danny.

Just then, Mum shouted from downstairs. 'Danny! Matthew! There's *another* Wibberley Wobberley wagon outside, and the driver says the whole delivery's for you!'

'Cool!' said Matt as they dashed downstairs. 'That lot'll fill your garage!'

'The garage is *already* full of the stuff,' said Mum. 'Danny, these jelly-records have got to stop.'

'But we need that many for the Longest Mexican Jelly-wave in a Sports Stadium attempt,' he explained. 'We'll fill the stands at Penleydale United with jellies, give them a poke at one end, and send a wave right the way round. It'll be the last one, I promise.'

At that moment there was a screech of disgust from upstairs.

'Mum!' yelled Natalie. 'I've got to get ready for my dance competition and Danny's filled the bath with jelly!'

Danny, Matthew and Mum
went upstairs and looked in
through the bathroom
door.

'Tell him!' wailed Natalie.

'I'm telling you, Danny,'
said Mum. 'You're going to
need a bigger bath!'

Danny and Matthew stood outside
the changing rooms at school as
the Bunbury Bantams' minibus
pulled up. Danny was wearing a
Walchester United scarf around his
face, in case Sally Butterworth had
any kissing in mind. He pulled it
tighter.

'Hiya, Matt,' beamed Sally,
racing from the bus and slapping him hard on the
shoulder. 'Hiya, Dan. Are you playing today?'

'No, I'm not quite fit yet. Just a few more days.'

'So who's in goal?'

Before Danny could answer, a voice snarled, 'Butterworth!'

Sally spun round. 'Potts!' she growled.

Everyone stopped what they were doing. Footballs rolled away unkicked. Conversations stopped in mid-sentence. Parents and children craned their necks to see what was happening. Those standing between Sally and Maradona moved aside quickly, and the pair faced each other down two long lines of hushed, tense children. A gust of wind sent an empty packet of crisps skittering across the desert of tarmac that separated the two opponents.

Sally advanced slowly and menacingly towards Maradona, looking like a volcano about to erupt.

'You're useless, Butterworth,' sneered Maradona, jabbing his finger at her. '*You* won't score today, because *I'm* in goal.'

Sally glowered. 'I know your weakness,

Potts,' she said. 'You won't stop me.'

Maradona snorted and pushed past her towards the changing rooms.

'So, have you two met before?' grinned Matthew.

'Potts used to play for us,' replied Sally. 'He bullied my best friend, Vicky, and forced her off the team. We all hated him. We scored an own goal against him on purpose, just to stop him breaking the record for most clean sheets.'

'He's pretty good,' said Danny. 'You might not score against him today.'

'He's not as good as you, Dan, and I've scored against you.'

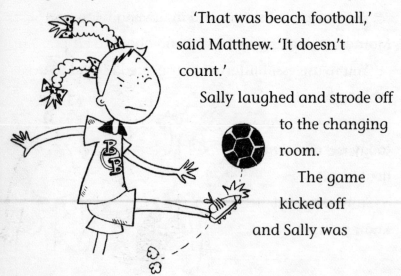

'That was beach football,' said Matthew. 'It doesn't count.'

Sally laughed and strode off to the changing room.

The game kicked off and Sally was

unstoppable. Matthew tried to mark her, but she ran him ragged. After only five minutes, she got the ball about fifteen metres from the Sparrows' goal, dummied Matthew, glanced up and saw Potts still on his line. She curled a shot high past his outstretched hand, into the corner of the net.

Danny didn't know how to feel. Sally had scored against Potts (Ace!), but she had also scored against his team (Not Ace!).

As Potts went to pick the ball out of the net, he began to limp. Five more times Sally beat him, and set up goals for three more of her team. With every goal scored, Maradona's limp got worse, and on the touchline his father's face turned more and more purple. As Potts picked the ball out of his goal for the tenth time, the final whistle blew. He staggered towards the touchline like a pirate with a wooden leg.

'You were useless!' screamed his father.

'I was injured,' complained Potts. 'I hurt my leg at the start. She wouldn't have scored *any* if I'd been OK.'

The Sparrows' coach shook his head. 'I'm sorry, Maradona. That girl's obviously got you beat and we're playing them again in the first round of the Invitation Tournament.' He looked at Danny. 'Make sure you're match-fit by next week, Dan. I want you back in the team!'

The Wibbly Wobbly Wonder

It was the day of the Mexican Jelly-wave. In the home team's changing room at Penleydale Town, the communal jacuzzi bath was full to the brim with gently bubbling orange jelly: quick-setting Pineapple and Parsnip added to Peach and Pickled-onion flavour. The air burbling up from the bottom of the big bath stirred the jelly perfectly.

Matthew had come up with a formula to calculate how *many* jellies they would need and how *much* jelly-mix they would have to make up:

TSA of T ÷ ASA of BJM = TN of JN → WWW × AV of JM = TA of JN (Total Surface Area of the Terraces, divided by the Average Surface Area of the Bottom of the Jelly Moulds = Total Number of Jellies Needed to Produce the Wibbly Wobbly Wonder, times the Average Volume of the Jelly Moulds = Total Amount of Jelly Needed).

'We'll need eight thousand eight hundred and twenty-three jellies,' Matthew explained. 'At an average of three point four litres per mould, we'll have to mix twenty-nine thousand nine hundred and ninety-eight point two litres of jelly, which is almost exactly one and a half big bathfuls.'

'If you say so, Matt,' said Danny.

Mr Eckersley, the club groundsman, had cleared out a storeroom and found a pile of dusty silver cups from Penleydale Town's Golden Years, 1923–1936, when trophies came thick and fast. They made perfect jelly moulds and now stood in rows along the edge of the jacuzzi.

Every member of the Coalclough Sparrows football team pitched in. Some poured the liquid into the cups, while others carried the set jellies out to the terraces, where Danny and Matthew carefully placed them in rows, making sure that they all touched each other. After hours of hard work, two and a half sides of the ground were full of transparent orange trophy-shaped domes.

A large group of spectators had gathered in the centre of the pitch, including a photographer and reporter from the *Penleydale Clarion*. Danny and Matthew's parents had turned up to help the boys and to watch the wave.

Matthew nudged Danny. 'Look out, Sally Butterwart's arrived,' he whispered.

'Hiya, boys!' called Sally. 'I've got something special for *you*, Dan.' She presented Danny with a pink box decorated with a huge shiny pink ribbon.

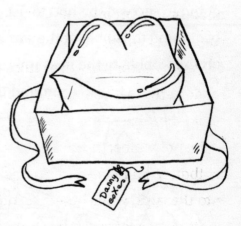

He lifted the lid and peeked inside. The box contained a big red lip-shaped jelly. Danny glanced nervously at Matthew. 'Er . . . thanks Sally,' he mumbled. 'Um . . . what flavour is it?'

Sally smiled. 'Passion fruit.'

Danny gulped, and quickly put the lid back on the box.

'Aren't you going to try it?' she asked.

'Er . . . yeah . . . maybe later. I know. I'll put it in with the others. We need all the jellies we can get for the wobble-wave.'

Sally gently placed the jelly-lips in the centre of the stand, and Danny and Matthew filled up the space around them.

At last all four stands were full. If Danny was going to succeed, he had to get all the jellies at the beginning to wibble at the same time and pass on the wobble to the next row, and so on right around the ground. Matthew checked his Multiple Coordinated Jelly-wobble Starting Device: a contraption

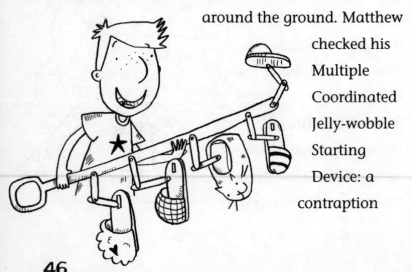

made of wood, springs and old slippers that would, at the pull of a lever, set the Mexican Jelly-wave in motion.

'It's ready,' announced Matthew.

Danny flexed his fingers, stood in front of the device, and the countdown began.

'Five . . . four . . . three . . . two . . . one . . . GO!'

Danny yanked the lever. All the way up the concrete steps of the Walter Widget Stand, the slippers flipped over, each one slapping simultaneously, with a wonderful wet whack, into the first jelly on each row. The wobble-wave spread with amazing speed along the terrace, around the first bend, and across the Stubbins' Sticky Buns End behind the goal.

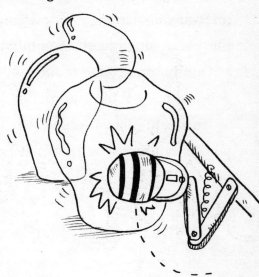

'Ace!' yelled Danny.

'Cool!' shouted Matthew.

'Go, wobble, go!' screamed Sally.

The crowd roared as the ripple raced around the next corner and charged down the Donkey Lane Stand, heading towards the red jelly-lips.

And that was when it all went horribly wrong.

Sally's jelly was thicker, the lips less floppy, and didn't transmit the wobble. The rhythm was ruined and chaos spread through the jellies like an infection. Soon  they were wibbling and wobbling in all directions.

Danny spun round to face Sally. 'Your lips have wrecked my wobble!' he cried.

'You should have eaten the jelly, like I wanted you to!' countered Sally. 'And when I score against you tomorrow, I'll wreck your clean-sheet record too.'

'Yeah?'

'Yeah! I've already scored against you, and this time it won't be just beach football!' Sally stomped off towards the exit. 'Urrgh! Boys!'

By now, the random, uncontrolled wobbling of the jellies had reached crisis point. Row by row they tumbled forward in a huge jelly cascade that went on and on until every single one had been deposited in a quivering orange pile, right around the touchline. Only Sally's wobble-proof lips remained in place.

Mr Eckersley stormed up to the boys. 'Look at all this mess on my grass,' he fumed. 'We've got the tournament tomorrow. What are you going to do about this jelly?'

Danny and Matthew gazed around the ground.

'Eat it?' suggested Danny.

Sally Versus Danny

Next day, the jelly still lay around the pitch like a glistening orange moat.

The Bunbury Bantams arrived, but their manager looked unhappy. 'The team's been hit by an outbreak of the Bunbury Burping Bug,' he complained as he got off the bus. 'We've had to bring a load of substitutes.'

Sally Butterworth, however, was burp-free and strode past Danny and Matthew without a second glance or a single, 'Hiya!'

'It was worth missing out on the Mexican Jelly-wave record just to shut Salty Buttybum up,' commented Matthew.

Danny frowned. 'It won't be worth it if she scores past me today,' he said. 'Sally's good. *And* she's mad.'

The first game of the tournament pitched

Coalclough Sparrows against Bunbury Bantams. Danny didn't have to save a single shot. He leaned against his post, watching, while his team slaughtered the weakened Bantams. Sally Butterworth was well marked by Matthew and she rarely touched the ball.

Then, with three minutes left and the Sparrows winning eight–nil, Sally broke free. Dodging desperate tackles, she cut through the defence and was through with just Danny to beat. Memories of their last goalmouth clash flooded Danny's brain.

As Sally charged towards him, he repeated, 'Beach football doesn't count,  beach football doesn't count, beach football doesn't count.'

He moved out to narrow the angle as Sally lifted her right foot to shoot. Only *this* time she dragged the ball to her left and shimmied past him. Danny dived and lunged at her feet, but she was too fast and dodged round him.

It was an open goal. His clean-sheet record was surely gone.

Danny sprawled on the grass, saw Sally look up at the empty net, pull back her left foot, and blast the ball . . . *over the bar*!

She stood for a moment staring at the open goal, then turned and winked at Danny. 'I missed,' she said. 'Looks like the record's yours.'

There was a commotion in the stands as Maradona Potts and his father shoved their way through the spectators, down to the touchline.

'They cheated!' yelled Potts. 'She missed on purpose!'

Danny was furious – he didn't want Sally's help and would *never* cheat to break a record. He scooped up a handful of jelly from the sidelines and launched it at his rival. Potts ducked and the missile whizzed over his head and splattered all over Mr Potts instead.

'You're useless, Baker!' snarled Maradona.

His face disappeared in a gooey orange splodge.

'*I'm* not,' crowed Matthew. 'I'm the Puddlethorpe Junior Cowpat-chucking Champion.'

The other kids on the pitch seized their chance, and Maradona 'The Cheatboy' Potts and his bullying dad vanished under a barrage of jelly-bombs. The pair skulked out of the ground to the cheers of everyone there, and the sticky battle began. Soon the Three Hills Stadium resounded with the split and splat of hundreds of jelly-missiles. Danny's mum and dad joined in gleefully. Word of the hullabaloo spread to the changing rooms, and players from the other six teams in the tournament poured on to the grass to join in the fun.

The referee stood on the centre spot and gave a fierce blast on his whistle. Everyone froze.

'This game is abandoned!' he yelled. 'The *tournament* is abandoned! This ground is unsafe for football!' He picked up a handful of jelly and hurled it at Mr Eckersley. 'But the conditions are perfect for a jelly-fight! Play on!'

The rumpus rumbled on and soon the entire pitch became a springy orange mess. When at last the referee blew his whistle to call a halt to it, Sally squelched over to Danny and Matthew. 'Pity the game was called off,' she said. 'You would've broken the record for keeping a clean sheet.'

'Did you miss on purpose?' asked Danny.

Sally laughed and winked at him again. 'Give me a kiss and I'll tell you.'

'No way!' replied Danny, pulling his goalkeeper's jersey up over his face.

'Then I'm not telling.' Sally turned and headed towards the changing rooms.

Danny nodded his head. 'She did.'

Matthew shook his head. 'She didn't.'

'We'll never know.'

'Not unless you kiss her.'

'Urggghhhhh! Gross!' cried Danny.

'Yeah! Mega-*giga*-gross!' agreed Matthew.

Danny Baker - Record Breaker

Dear Mr Bibby

I didn't manage to get the Mexican Jelly-wave
all the way round the Three Hills Stadium. It was
going well until the wobble hit Sally Butterworth's
lips. Then all the other jellies went
crazy and the whole lot ended up
on the touchline.

stupid lips

But it was great ammunition for the massive
Pineapple and Parsnip and Peach and Pickled-

jelly

onion Jelly Fight I started the
next day! At the height of the
battle, there were 487 people
chucking jelly at each other. It
was Ace! Every bit of grass turned
orange!

We were on the telly, and luckily someone from Creepy Crawly Creek Home for Rescued Invertebrates saw the news report. They were suffering a serious shortage of slime in their giant-worm enclosure and our jelly was just the thing they needed to put it right! They sent a big tanker-lorry, sucked all the jelly into it with a huge vacuum-cleaner pipe, and took it back to Bugsby Tyke in Yorkshire.

slime

We were winning eight-nil when the battle started, but the referee abandoned the game, so I couldn't break the clean-sheet record after all. But did we break a record with our jelly-fight?

Best wishes
Danny Baker

PS NEWSFLASH!!! Good thing I didn't post my letter this morning, because tonight I'm

hoping I finally got the record for the Most
Consecutive Games without Conceding a Goal,
when we beat the Dumdown Dewdrops two-nil.
Matthew's done the maths and it's actually
fifty-two games or 3,128 minutes. Have I done it?

The Great Big Book
of World Records
London

ARE YOU A RECORD
BREAKER?

Dear Danny

Bad luck with the Mexican Jelly-wave attempt, but *double congratulations* too!

Congratulations No. 1: You and the other 486 jelly-chuckers are record breakers! You beat the previous Mass Jelly-fight in a Sports Stadium world record by 244 people. I wish I'd been there to see *that* record broken! I'm sending you a separate parcel with all the other certificates. Could you please hand them out to everyone who took part in the record?

Congratulations No. 2: You have played the Most Consecutive Number of Games without Conceding a Goal. This is a truly awesome feat. Your dad must be very proud of you.

Best wishes

Eric Bibby

Keeper of the Records

PS How on earth did Sally Butterworth's lips get in the way of the wave? Was she trying to eat the jelly when the wobble hit her?

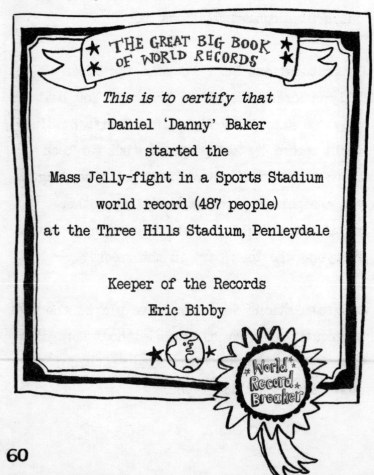

THE GREAT BIG BOOK OF WORLD RECORDS

This is to certify that
Daniel 'Danny' Baker
started the
Mass Jelly-fight in a Sports Stadium
world record (487 people)
at the Three Hills Stadium, Penleydale

Keeper of the Records
Eric Bibby

World Record Breaker

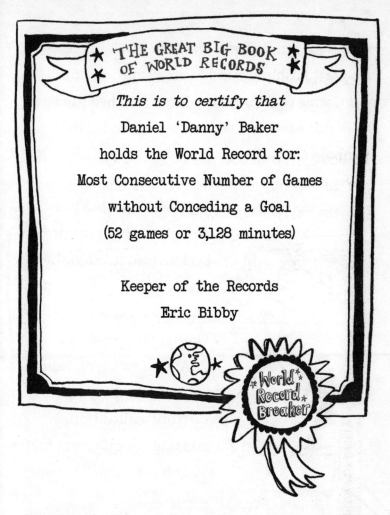

THE GREAT BIG BOOK OF WORLD RECORDS

This is to certify that
Daniel 'Danny' Baker
holds the World Record for:
Most Consecutive Number of Games
without Conceding a Goal
(52 games or 3,128 minutes)

Keeper of the Records
Eric Bibby

World Record Breaker

Danny, Matthew and Dad were in the back garden
trying to break the Group Keepy-uppy Headers with
a Jelly Football world record. Matthew had been
tinkering with the mix and he was sure he'd finally

got it right: three parts Winkle and Whortleberry, two parts Raspberry and Roast Potato, and one part Cockle and Cumquat. Mum watched from the bench beneath the tree as she mended the lawnmower.

The attempt was going well. The jelly football wibbled, but not too much. It wobbled, but just enough to give it bounce. Dad headed it to Matthew: 'Twenty-three . . .' counted Matt and headed it to Danny. 'Twenty-four . . .'

At that moment, Natalie walked into the garden.

'Nats!' called Danny, nodding the quivering ball towards his sister. 'On your head!'

SPLAT!!!

'Mum!' screeched Natalie, as the purple jelly slid down her hair and on to her shoulders. 'Tell them!'

Mum shook her head and looked thoughtful. 'I think we need more Winkle.'

The Great Big Book
of World Records
London

Dear Danny

ARE YOU A RECORD
BREAKER ?

Following your recent jelly exploits, I
thought you would be interested to know
that 'Wibberley Wobberley – the Jellies from
Mobberley' are now officially world-beaters!
Scientists from *The Great Big Book of World
Records* have checked their jellies with a
Wibblewobbleometer, and I can now declare
that they are officially the World's Wibbliest
Wobbliest Jellies!

The company has a fascinating history. In 1835,
the town of Mobberley in Cheshire was bathed
in delicious aromas, as two friends, Wilberforce
Wibberley and Waldorf Wobberley, opened a
small jelly factory on Pigsfoot Lane. They sold
their special, exotic home-made jellies from The

Wibberley Wobberley Jelly and Sewing Machine
Emporium on the High Street, and quickly
gained a reputation for producing the wibbliest
and wobbliest jellies in England. Unfortunately
their sewing machines were considered to make
the wibbliest wobbliest *clothes* in England,
so the friends made the excellent decision
to forget all about sewing machines and
concentrate on jelly-making. I for one am glad
they did!

In 1838, the friends opened the Mobberley
Medicinal Jelly Baths. People travelled
from all over the world to 'take the jelly
wallow'. The company's vast range of herbal
jellies became famous for curing all sorts of
conditions, such as Lubbock's Lumbago, Gumboot
Gout and Seriously Spotty Bottom Syndrome.

The company's big break came in 1840, when
Wilberforce Wibberley sent Queen Victoria a
box of Bratwurst and Strawberry-flavoured

jelly to celebrate her marriage to the German Prince Albert. Her Majesty was *very* amused, and declared the jelly to be 'the most wobblesome food I have ever tasted'. The Queen liked the treat so much, that 'Wibberley Wobberley – the Jellies from Mobberley' became official suppliers of jelly to the Crown.

The jellies wibbled and wobbled to every part of the British Empire. During the Crimean War, Colonel Fortesque Ponsonby-Fflip, Commander of the 1st (and Last) Ponsonby Peashooter Regiment, said his army 'marched on their jellies'. It was true! They filled their boots with Wibberley Wobberley Mushy-pea flavour to keep their feet warm!

In May 1854, the 3rd Battalion 379th Regiment of the Lordy Lordy Lowland Artillery ran out of cannonballs during the Battle of Umskidazi. Luckily the regimental cook had just made up a batch of extra wobbly Roast Beef and

Yorkshire Pudding jellies, and the gunners used these instead. The Russian army surrendered immediately so that they could eat the yummy sweet.

The year 1923 was the darkest in the company's history. A mysterious contamination of the jelly vats in the factory caused the jellies to lose their famous wibble. The company's deadly rivals, 'Jiggly Juggly – the Jellies from Buggly', were suspected of foul play, but nothing could be proved. People stopped buying Wibberley Wobberley, and although the jellies eventually got their wibble back, sales never recovered.

However, in 1992, Millie Wibberley and Molly Wobberley, Wilberforce and Waldorf's great-great-great-granddaughters, brought the company back to life. They began to invent uniquely weird and wonderful mixes, and sponsored the first Mobberley Jelly-spring

Marathon. They also supported the British Jelly-juggling team that won the world championships five years in a row. Now, with the award of 'The World's Wibbliest Wobbliest Jellies', I am delighted to officially announce that 'Wibberley Wobberley – the Jellies from Mobberley' are back on top of the world!

Best wishes

Eric Bibby

Keeper of the Records

DANNY BAKER RECORD BREAKER

The Lemon-Puff Peril

WARNING!
DANGER AT
THE DEEP
END

Summer's End Saturday

To The Keeper of the Records
The Great Big Book of World Records
London

Dear Mr Bibby

Yesterday I attempted the Continuous Musical Armpit-farting record. I managed to play 2,081 verses of 'Old MacDonald Had a Farm' on my left armpit, and had been going for fourteen hours, twenty-seven minutes and eleven seconds, when I squeezed too hard on the 2,081st 'Eee-I-Eee-I-Oh' and bruised my fingers.

My sister, Natalie, said that if I'd gone on any

longer, she'd have bruised
more than my fingers! She was
upstairs, trying to listen to her

favourite boy band, Boy$!!! (or Yawn$!!! as I call
them). Even with the volume turned right up,
she could still hear my armpit farts! Could they
have been the Loudest Ever?

Best wishes
Danny Baker

PS Matthew made a recording of my armpit
music on his dad's old tape recorder. It filled
nearly eight tapes.
I've sent one of
them with this letter.

The Great Big Book
of World Records
London

ARE YOU A RECORD
BREAKER ?

Dear Danny

I hope your bruised fingers aren't too painful
and don't affect your goalkeeping.

Your Continuous Musical Armpit-farting
performance was truly enchanting, but did not
trump that of the self-styled 'Grand Master of
Armpit-farting' Ronan O'Kidney, of Ballybogey
in Northern Ireland. On 19 and 20 August 2001,
Ronan played a selection of Irish folk-songs on
his left armpit for forty-two hours, fourteen
minutes and seven seconds, before repetitive
strain injury finally took its toll.

Ronan's armpit-farts were so loud he drowned
out the Ballybogey Boogie-woogie Bugle Boys,
who were playing in the village hall two

75

streets away, and forced them to cancel their concert!

Mr O'Kidney has written a concerto for Solo Armpit and Woodwind, but no traditional musicians will perform it with him. He is determined that the world should take armpit-music seriously and in 2007 formed the All-Ireland Armpit Orchestra, the first and only one of its kind. You could form an armpit band at your school and do duets with Matthew!

Good luck with your next record attempt.

Best wishes
Eric Bibby
Keeper of the Records

Danny stood on the wide flat sands of Bladderpool, with his bare feet in a small barrel of donkey do-do, holding a bunch of carrots in each hand. He was not alone. Two long lines of boys and girls also stood in barrels of donkey do-do forming an avenue that led off the sands and along the promenade.

They were all there to perform the Donkey Dung Dance on Bladderpool's Summer's End Saturday. All summer long the donkeys had paraded up and down the beach in their specially decorated straw hats, giving rides to happy children. Today was the day everyone thanked them for their hard work, before the animals went off to have a well-earned rest in their winter pasture. Crowds of people cheered and clapped as

77

a brass band, jugglers and acrobats escorted the donkeys between the lines of jiggling kids.

Danny waved the carrots around his head and boogied in the barrel.

'Come on, Matt,' he said, pointing to an unoccupied barrel of donkey dung. 'Get your shoes and socks off, grab some carrots and get dancing!'

'No thanks, Dan,' replied Matthew. 'I'd rather *chuck* poo than dance in it! Besides, I can see what it's doing to your feet.'

Danny glanced down and his eyes widened with delight. When the donkey parade had passed by, the boys raced over to where Danny's mum and sister, Natalie, were waiting.

'Danny! It looks like you're wearing brown socks!' exclaimed Mum. 'And your toes are like little shiny conkers!'

Natalie's nose wrinkled in disgust. 'I'm not sitting in a car all the way back to Penleydale with *those filthy feet*!'

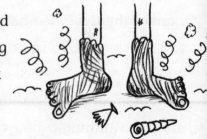

'Will it come off?' asked Matthew.

'There's no way they'll let you in the pool for Swimming Club tomorrow if it doesn't,' smirked Natalie.

Mum examined Danny's blotchy feet. 'When *I* was your age, I did the Donkey Dung Dance. My grandma got my feet clean by soaking them in vinegar and water, then rubbing them with newspaper. If you do it twice a day, the stains should be gone by next weekend.'

'Aw, Mum!' moaned Natalie. 'The house'll smell like a fish and chip shop!'

'Ace!' said Danny.

'Cool!' agreed Matthew.

Mum was right. By the following Sunday morning, Danny's toes were back in the pink. The boys set off to the Sports Centre for their weekly session with the Penleydale Sea Squirts Swimming Club, both carrying bright-blue flippers under their arms.

Natalie walked on ahead of them. She was in the county swimming team, something that she never let her brother forget, because Danny hadn't even swum a length yet. He had never managed to pass the red line that marked the end of the shallow water and the beginning of the Deep End.

'I really want to try for my twenty-five metres certificate next week,' Danny told Matthew.

'Do you think you can Cross The Line?'

'Yeah, I *have* to! I want to have a proper look at The Grid.'

The Grid was a metal filter in the wall at the deep end that sucked the water through and kept it clean. From the surface of the pool, it looked like a huge, gaping mouth, with clumps of hair and old sticking plasters dangling from its teeth.

'Willy Williams in Year Six told me that his cousin's best-friend's older sister swam too close to The Grid and got *eaten alive*!' said Danny.

'I never heard *that* one,' replied Matthew. 'But I *did* hear there's a monster python that lives in the drains behind it! It escaped from Dooley's Pet Shop fifty years ago and just kept growing. They say it's probably the biggest in the world by now!'

Danny laughed. 'That reminds me, I've had an idea for a new record attempt. My feet went all wrinkly and crinkly when I was soaking the donkey do-do off last week. How long do you think I'd have to sit in water for that to happen to my *whole body*?'

'No way,' gasped Matthew. 'You're not thinking about . . . ?'

'Oh yes I am,' confirmed Danny.

He rummaged in his pocket and pulled out a crumpled-up piece of paper. It was a newspaper clipping with a picture of a strange-looking gadget. He handed it to Matthew. 'Can you make one of these?'

'What is it?'

'A Wrinkleometer.' Danny pointed to the different parts on the diagram. 'The small wheel measures the length of the wrinkles, the flat bit that looks like a little ruler checks the depth, and the two pointy things are to count the wrinkles per centimetre.'

Matthew nodded. 'Yeah, I'll have a go. It'll take me a few days though.'

'That's OK. Today we're going to put these flippers to good use and try to break another record.'

'Just you and me?'

'No, *all* the Sea Squirts – the more we have flipping, the better.'

Danny and Matthew approached the corner of Tempest Road. The Sports Centre stood at the top, right opposite the Crumbly Crunch biscuit factory. It was time for a quick game of Guess What Biscuit Is Baking Today.

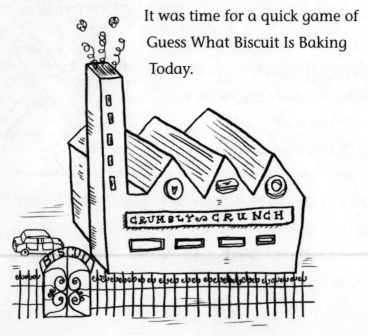

CRUMBLY CRUNCH

'Chocolate bourbons,' predicted Danny.

'Ginger nuts,' guessed Matthew.

As they turned the corner, the smell of baking biscuits wafted to them on the breeze. Danny and Matthew sniffed deeply.

'Custard creams!' they laughed, and made their way down the road to the Sports Centre.

Wet Pants

Dear Mr Bibby

Yesterday, twenty-one kids from my swimming club, the Penleydale Sea Squirts, tried to break a record. We all lined up at the shallow end of the pool, and at my signal everyone flipped their flippers at the same time.

A small ripple rolled down the pool, hit the wall at the far end, and bounced back. As it reached us we flipped again and made the ripple bigger.

Each time it came back to us we flipped, and each time the wave got bigger and faster. With one final flip at exactly the right moment, we created a huge monster of a wave.

It was Ace! The water crashed over the far end, swept through the doors of the girls' changing rooms, then out across the reception area and into Tempest Road. Natalie said we were being childish and wouldn't join in. She was in the changing rooms as the wave passed through. It picked her up, carried her outside and dumped her on the pavement. She wasn't pleased.

The water travelled 354 m before running out of steam just before the zebra crossing near the Post Office.

Matthew found out that the pool holds 562,500 litres of water. If you take away the 26,373 litres of water left behind after the wave, this means that we managed to empty 536,127 litres of water from the pool.

Are we the Swimming Pool Emptying Champions of the World?

Best wishes

Danny Baker

PS I've got a verruca. My dad told me he once had five on one foot and two on the other, at *the same time!* What's the world record for having the most verrucas? I can't try to break the record, because Mum's covered my toe in Verrucablaster! cream. She says verrucas are banned when our new baby arrives.

The Great Big Book
of World Records
London

ARE YOU A RECORD
BREAKER ?

Dear Danny

I'm sorry, but the Penleydale Sea Squirts are
not record breakers. The record for Collective
Emptying of a Swimming Pool by Simultaneous
Flipper-action is held by thirty-three members
of the Freemantle Flipper-floppers Formation
Water-dancing Team, of Freemantle, Australia.

On 24 December 1996 they displaced 1,967,852
litres of water from their pool. The Team Coach
asked them to do it because his glass eye had
dropped out into the water and no one could
find it. The plan worked and the Flipper-
floppers eventually discovered the glass eye
staring up at them from the bottom of the deep
end.

Bad luck with your record attempt, Danny. I
hope the other children in the Sea Squirts
won't be too disappointed. It sounds like you
all had fun!

In answer to your second question, the world
record for Most Verrucas is 993, held by Lars
von Doinker, of Molde in Norway. He has size
seventeen feet, so has lots of room to grow them.
Mr von Doinker believes that verrucas are an
alien life form, come to take over the world
foot by foot, and that he is their leader.

So if you want to save the world, keep using
the Verrucablaster! cream!

Best wishes
Eric Bibby
Keeper of the Records

Danny pulled on his waterproof tracksuit bottoms, gathered the material together just above his left ankle, twisted the cloth tightly, and tied it in a firm knot. He repeated the procedure with his right trouser leg and then walked round to the side of the house where Dad kept the hosepipe.

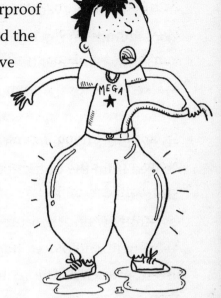

Danny pushed the end of the hose into the top of his trousers, and Matthew turned on the tap. Cold water gushed in and the trousers ballooned out, tight and taut, like two big blue sausages.

Danny gasped. 'Why couldn't we use warm water?'

'Because I read that swimming records are more likely to get broken if the pool water's cold,' replied Matthew. 'So, it might be the same with Water-filled-trousers Land-speed Dashing.'

'If you say so, Matt,' said Danny. 'But I've got goosebumps on my legs as big as gobstoppers!'

Danny tightened the belt around his waist and walked towards the front of the house. His legs were heavy with the weight of water, and he had to swing each one forward to move. Thin trickles leaked from the trouser bottoms and seeped into his trainers.

Matthew had measured out fifty metres of pavement and placed flags at each end. He checked his stopwatch as Danny took up position at the end of the street.

'On your marks . . . get set . . . go!'

Danny shuffled stiffly down the street, trying to get his running-rhythm right. As he passed the finish line, Matthew stopped the watch and read the display: 51.26 seconds.

'I can do better than that!' said Danny, gasping for air.

He got his breath back and prepared to do a second run. This time, he cut his time to 38.91 seconds.

'I can go faster,' he puffed. 'One more try.'

'Go!' called Matthew, and Danny got off to a great start, really picking up speed. This was going to be the fastest run, he could tell.

Suddenly, about twenty metres into the dash, Natalie and her best friends Kaylie and Kylie rushed down the garden path and surrounded him. They each had a pair of nail clippers, and held them up for Danny to see.

'*Noooooooooooooooo!*' wailed Danny, as he realized what they were about to do.

The three girls attacked Danny's trousers with the nail clippers, snipping dozens of tiny holes in the fabric. Thin spurts of water shot from the little punctures and in moments Danny's trouser legs were leaking like a sieve.

'That's for dropping jelly on me and spoiling my hair!' shouted Kaylie.

'That's for putting jelly in my sleeping bag and making me blotchy!' yelled Kylie.

'And that's for . . . *everything*!' shrieked Natalie. 'You should be happy – now you've got world-record-breaking leaky pants!'

The girls retreated into the house, cackling like witches.

'Matt, I've been ambushed!' cried

Danny, standing in a steadily growing puddle of water. 'Get the sticky tape, quick!'

Crossing
The Line

Dear Mr Bibby

Natalie and her friends sabotaged my attempt
on the Water-filled-trousers Land-speed Dash
record, by puncturing my pants. My best speed
was only 4.626 km/h before they got me, and I
know this isn't even close to the record. When
I've mended the pants, I'll have another go. I
might even attempt the Water-filled-trousers
Long-distance Dawdle record. I'll just do it as
far away from Nats as possible. How far do
I need to dawdle to be a
record breaker?

Best wishes
Danny Baker

yuck!
← girls

The Great Big Book
of World Records
London

Dear Danny

That was a good try – 4.626 km/h is fast for
a Water-filled-trousers Land-speed Dash, but
the record is held by Deng Dong of Hong Kong,
who reached 15.3 km/h wearing specially made
aerodynamic dash-pants.

The record for Water-filled-trousers Long-
distance Dawdling is humongous. It is held by
Tebogo Selepeng of Botswana, who dawdled the
entire 1,750-km length of the Limpopo River in
Africa. It took him 191 days.

Dawdling at night because it was cooler,
Tebogo topped up his trousers from the edge
of the river. When he reached the end of his
gargantuan trek, his pants were swarming with

tadpoles of the Lesser-spotted Limpopo Trouser Frog. This tiny amphibian was thought to be extinct because its spawn can only hatch in the trousers of fishermen who wade into the water, and nowadays the local fishermen always use boats.

As Tebogo paddled into the river to release the tadpoles from his trousers, he discovered *why* the fishermen use boats – he and all the tadpoles in his pants were gobbled up by a huge hungry crocodile. Now, both Tebogo Selepeng and the Lesser-spotted Limpopo Trouser Frog are *definitely* extinct.

Best wishes
Eric Bibby
Keeper of the Records

Danny and Matthew leaned into the gusting wind as they walked into town, heading for the Sports Centre.

'This weather's perfect for flying a kite,' said Danny.

'Yeah,' agreed Matthew. 'Let's go up to Miggin's Mop this afternoon. You could try for the Highest Kite-flying world record.'

Danny shook his head. 'Not today. I'm going to stay in the pool until closing-time. Now that you've made the Wrinkleometer, I want to have a go at the Whole-body Skin-wrinkles world record.'

They approached the top of Tempest Road.

'Cow biscuits?' wondered Danny.

'Garibaldis?' suggested Matthew.

The boys rounded the corner and sucked the gorgeous smell from the biscuit factory up their nostrils.

'Oaty bobnobs!'

Once inside the Sports Centre, they got changed and entered the pool. Matthew kept walking towards the Deep End, to be with the strong swimmers and big kids. Danny remained at the shallow end, where the weak swimmers and the little kids were. His white, rubbery Verrucablaster! Containment Sock squeezed his left foot uncomfortably.

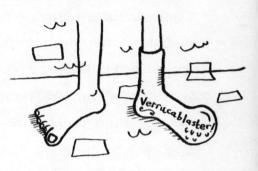

Danny lowered himself into the cold water, took a deep breath and swam a slow but determined width across the pool.

'Well done, kiddo!' shouted Trevor, the instructor. 'You're getting better every week.'

Danny kept glancing over at Matthew and Natalie as the good swimmers practised their racing dives. He wanted to join them *so* much.

Natalie noticed Danny looking. She stuck her tongue out at him, then made fun of his swimming by pretending to doggy-paddle.

That did it: he *had* to Cross The Line and swim to The Grid.

Danny launched himself from the end of the pool and began to swim towards the Deep End. As he reached halfway, he sensed the deep water below him and started to panic. His head went under the surface and he came up spluttering and coughing.

The end of a long white pole appeared in front of him and Danny grabbed it gratefully. From the edge of the pool, Trevor guided him back to the shallow water.

'Good try, kiddo,' he said. 'Have a rest and stay down this end. I don't want to have to rescue you a second time.'

Danny stood in the water at the side of the pool and got his breath back.

Matthew swam over to him. 'Hey, Dan, guess what I've just heard? Tiggy Jenkins told me that our flipper-wave washed all the sticky gloop out of the plugholes in the girls' showers. The caretaker shovelled it into a big pile and it's still there! Tiggy's sister said it's gross!'

'Ace!' replied Danny, cheering up at once. 'Let's go and take a look!'

The boys climbed out of the pool and sauntered casually towards the entrance of the girls' changing rooms. Danny took a quick glance over his shoulder, checking that no one had noticed them.

'Now!' he said, darting through the door.

A horrible sight was waiting for them. The glistening black mass of slimy, hairy goo lurked in a dark corner by the lockers, like an alien killer blob.

'Ace,' breathed Danny.

'Cool,' agreed Matthew.

Danny examined it closely. 'This stuff's just what I need to make my woolly-mammoth model for history.'

He searched around for something to scoop it into, and his eyes fell on Natalie's spare swimming cap sticking out of her backpack.

'Perfect!'

Danny filled the cap with dollops of the greasy plughole gloop.

Just then, they heard the shrill 'peep' of Trevor's whistle.

'Come on!' urged Matthew. 'We've got to go back before they notice we've gone!'

Danny shoved the bulging hat into a large pocket of Natalie's bag and zipped it up quickly.

'I'll get it out later,' said Danny as the boys hurried out of the girls' changing room. He jumped back into the water. 'I'm going to hang around here for the rest of the day and get wrinkly.'

Matthew smiled. 'I'll come back around teatime with the Wrinkleometer at the ready!'

Prune

Dear Mr Bibby

Last Sunday I stayed almost all day in the shallow end of Penleydale Pool. I only got out to have a wee. I'd have stayed in even longer, but Mum sent Natalie to drag me out because my tea was ready.

By then, my whole body was like a big white prune. I've seen lots of prunes, because my Grandma Florrie eats them every day to keep her Regular, whatever that means.

my body

Matthew had made a Wrinkleometer to work out my Skin-wrinkle Index.

The deepest and longest wrinkle he found started

on my belly, stretched around my side, carried on over my bottom, down my left leg and stopped just above my left knee.

He used the Wrinkle-length Wheel Attachment to measure the wrinkle, and it was 91 cm long.

Then he used the Wrinkle-depth Dipstick Attachment, and found the wrinkle was 3.9 cm deep at one point.

The crinkliest wrinkle was under my chin. It was only 16.5 cm long, but when Matthew used the Wrinkle-crinkle Gauge, he said it had seven crinkles per centimetre, making 115.5 crinkles per wrinkle.

Wrinkle-ometer

wrinkles!

I had 574 separate wrinkles on my body.

Matthew worked out that my Skin-wrinkle Index was 367.

It took nearly one and a half hours to make all these measurements. My tea went cold, Mum says I'm grounded for a week (except for football practice), and I've got a really bad cold from sitting in the water so long.

Was it all worth it? Are my wrinkles the wrinkliest, crinkliest ever?

Best wishes
Danny Baker

The Great Big Book
of World Records
London

Dear Danny

I'm sorry to tell you that you've missed again!
It was an excellent attempt, but the world's
wrinkliest person is Thelma McCurdie, of
Kissimmee, Florida - the same Thelma McCurdie
who holds the world records for the biggest and
spottiest bottom!

Embarrassed by all the attention given to
her vast behind when she broke those records,
Thelma went on a crash diet to make it smaller.
Unfortunately, while she lost all the fat, she
didn't lose all the skin. After a year of living
on just celery and water, Thelma's whole body
looked like a huge, deflated hot-air balloon.

Her longest single wrinkle went five times

around her body, and measured 36.43 m.

Her crinkliest wrinkle had 2,973 crinkles per wrinkle.

Her Skin-wrinkle Index was a massive 3,769!

Her deepest wrinkle was 35.6 cm deep.

A team of specially trained officers from the Great Big Book of World Records went to check Thelma out. When they began to use the Wrinkle-depth Dipstick Attachment of the Wrinkleometer, in the deep folds of skin, they discovered:

A family of hamsters (two adults and five babies)
Three jelly beans
A baseball mitt
A French dictionary
Two sticks of half-eaten celery
A bunch of keys

and . . .

A three-month-old *TV Guide*

Yours was a brave attempt, Danny, but you
could *never* compete with Thelma's tent-sized
torso. I hope your cold gets better soon.

Best wishes
Eric Bibby
Keeper of the Records

Danny and Matthew were just leaving home to play the Tootleby Tomahawks in the Penleydale Cup when, from her bedroom, Natalie let out a horrible, blood-curdling scream.

Dad ran from the living room and bounded up the stairs. Danny and Matthew followed him.

Mum rushed out of the bathroom.

'Don't scream like that, Natalie!' she said. 'The shock made the baby jump in my bump!'

'There's a big black furry thing in my backpack!' cried Natalie.

The boys looked guiltily at each other.

'I forgot to take out the hairy gloop!' whispered Danny.

Dad went into the spare room. He returned wearing his motorcycle helmet and goalkeeping gloves, and wielding a cricket bat.

'Stand back,' he ordered, striding into Natalie's bedroom.

'Er . . . Dad . . .'

'Hush, Danny!' hissed his father, raising the bat above his head like a Samurai warrior.

'But, Dad, it's just a hatful of plughole gloop.'

'What?' spluttered his sister.

'From the drains at the swimming pool.'

'Mum!' yelled Natalie. 'Tell him!'

She made a lunge for Danny's ears, but the boys were too quick. They fled

down the stairs and out of the house.

As they made their way to the school, the air swirled with brown and yellow leaves, ripped from the trees by the strong wind.

Danny grinned. 'Next time I put yucky stuff in Nat's bag, remind me to take it out again!'

'Will do!' laughed Matthew. 'Hey, I saw your dad's photo in the paper!'

'Yeah, he's really chuffed to have Walchester United's new stand named after him. There's a sign across the front of the roof that says "The Bobby

Baker Stand" in letters two metres high. It's Ace!'

'I thought you had to be dead for a trillion years before you got something named after you, like . . .' Matthew thought for a moment. 'Saint Paul's Cathedral.'

'I wonder if I'll ever have something named after me.'

'A tin of smelly foot powder probably,' grinned Matthew.

They turned through the school gates. Danny ducked as a wrapper from a Crumbly Crunch Mint-choc Dreambar whizzed past his head.

'Did you break the Whole-body

CRUMBLY CRUNCH
♥ Mint - Choc
Dreambars ♥

Skin-wrinkles record?' asked Matthew.

'No! Guess who's got the certificate for *that* one?'

'Not Thelma "Big Bum" McCurdie?'

'Yeah! Her bottom's unbeatable,' complained Danny. 'Huge, spotty *and* wrinkled!'

Matthew sniffed. 'What's that smell?'

'It's not my feet!' said Danny, sniffing too. 'That's biscuits! The wind must be blowing it all the way from the Crumbly Crunch factory.'

'It's fruity flapjacks!' said Matthew.

'Nah, jammy sandwich!' argued Danny.

They both breathed in deeply through their noses, then nodded in agreement. 'Fig rolls!'

A Bad Attack of Wind

The Great Big Book
of World Records
London

Dear Danny

I hope you are well and planning your next record attempt. Unfortunately, I have some bad news: you are no longer the world record holder for the Most Saves in a Single Game.

Your record was broken by Giuseppe 'Peppe' Marulo, the goalkeeper for Atletico Tonino, a small club near Naples, in southern Italy. At half-time in a match against rivals Sant'Anna, nine of his team-mates went on strike and refused to carry on with the game because their traditional half-time pepperoni pizzas had not been delivered.

Peppe and the other remaining player had brought their own meatball sandwiches and played on, keeping the score to 39-nil. In doing so, Peppe made an incredible 109 saves, otherwise the score would have been 148-nil! (This would have been a world record, by the way.)

I'm sorry to disappoint you, Danny, but I thought you would prefer to know.

Best wishes
Eric Bibby
Keeper of the Records

'Hi, Dan!' said Matthew, running up the stairs and into Danny's bedroom.

'Hiya, Matt.' Danny held out Mr Bibby's letter for Matthew to read. 'My world record for the Most Saves in a Single Game has been beaten.'

'Never!' Matthew shook his head in disbelief and began to read.

'That's not fair!' he protested, when he had finished it. 'You didn't let *any* goals in. He let *thirty-nine* in!'

'He still made one hundred and nine saves,' said Danny. 'So he's the record holder. Dad says this always happens when you're the best at something: sooner or later someone comes along and takes your crown.'

'What are you going to do with the certificate?' asked Matthew.

'It's staying up there on the wall,' said Danny. 'And today I'm going to get my twenty-five metres swimming certificate to put up next to it.'

Matthew grinned. 'Come on, let's get to the pool.'

'Be careful, you two,' called Mum, as the boys

left the house. 'It's
so windy today you
might get blown
all the way to
Timbuktu.'

'What's the world
record for being
blown by the wind?'
wondered Danny as he
and Matthew staggered
down the High Street.

They leaned forward
into the fierce gale. Several times it blew them back
a pace or two. There was no need to wait until
they reached Tempest Road before guessing which
biscuits were baking today. The tangy-sweet smell
had been carried all over the town.

'Lemon puffs!' they cried together.

A strong gust of wind pushed them straight
through the doors of the Sports Centre, and as
Danny and Matthew entered the pool area, they
saw that the team for the Swimming Gala had

been pinned
on the
noticeboard.
Natalie was
studying it
as the boys
walked towards her.

'You're in, Matt,' she
shouted.

'Yes!' exclaimed Matthew.
'Come on, Dan, Cross The Line today and you
might be in the next team.'

Natalie smirked. 'Who knows, Dan, you might
even be in the *county* team one day, like me,' she
said. 'By the way, *I'm* Team Captain.'

The boys sniggered and saluted.

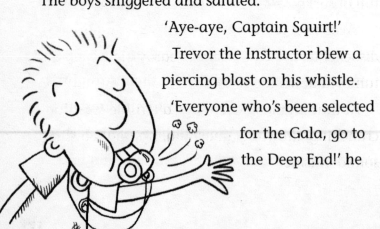

'Aye-aye, Captain Squirt!'

Trevor the Instructor blew a
piercing blast on his whistle.

'Everyone who's been selected
for the Gala, go to
the Deep End!' he

yelled, struggling to make himself heard above the howling wind.

Danny watched Matthew amble to the far end of the pool with the other team members.

'Well, kiddo,' shouted Trevor. 'Is today the day you're going to Cross The Line?'

'Definitely!' replied Danny.

'Good. Jump into the shallow end and I'll be back in a minute to help you.' Trevor strode away to speak to the team.

The ferocious wind screamed louder as the gale battered at Penleydale. Danny glanced out of the large window that ran the whole length of one side of the building. A green wheelie bin flew past, followed by a garden shed, a whole washing-line full of socks, and a policeman's helmet.

'Ace!' he exclaimed, his eyes widening in disbelief as two cars parked nearby blew over, and tumbled down the road.

At that moment, there was a terrible crashing, crunching, growling, gnashing, ripping, howling sound outside.

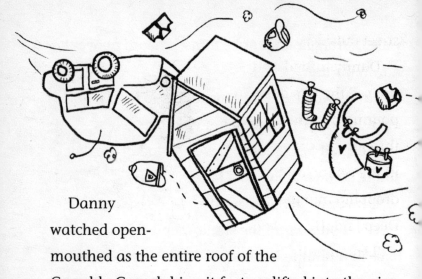

Danny watched open-mouthed as the entire roof of the Crumbly Crunch biscuit factory lifted into the air and spun away out of sight. Planks of wood, roof tiles, bits of paper and thousands of broken biscuits swirled and danced down Tempest Road.

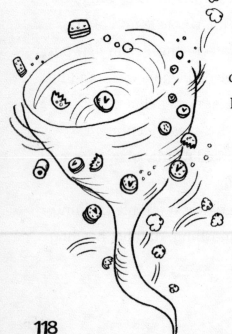

'IT'S A TORNADO!' he cried as a thick funnel of brilliant yellow powder whirled out of the factory and whizzed round the street outside.

Danny turned and noticed the fine dust pouring in torrents through the air vents in the ceiling and dropping into the Deep End. He sniffed.

'Lemon puffs!'

The Lemon-puff Peril

The Sea Squirts began to cry out, lost in the heavy, lemon-scented fog and sticky yellow water. The roof above them rattled and groaned as, outside, the tornado squealed and raged.

Danny jumped out of the shallow end and pushed the weak swimmers towards the exit.

'Go and get help,' he yelled. 'Tell someone to call the police and the fire brigade.'

He turned and stared down the pool in amazement. The thick, choking yellow cloud was billowing towards him. Danny took a deep breath and ran into it, towards the Deep End. He slipped and skidded in the slimy layer of lemon-puff paste that was forming along the edge of the pool. Suddenly, the squealing wind stopped as the tornado moved away, and Danny heard coughs, sneezes and cries for help coming from within the fog. He recognized Matthew's voice.

'Everyone over here!' he called, but his voice was lost amongst the cries of the other kids.

The farty-squelch of his Verrucablaster! Containment Sock sucking at the sticky paste on the floor gave Danny an idea. In desperation, he put his right hand into his left armpit and squeezed as hard as he could. The distinctive rubbery rasp of his armpit-fart echoed through the pool. He began pumping his arm over and over again and the familiar vibrating melody of 'Old MacDonald Had a Farm' cut through the lemon-puff smog.

'Danny! Is that you?' shouted Matthew.

'Yeah!' replied Danny. 'Follow the farts, Matt! Follow the farts!'

A few seconds later, Matthew struggled out of the water.

'It . . . tastes . . . great!' he exclaimed.

Danny laughed. 'If this had happened yesterday, it would have been chocolate-chip cookie!'

He continued playing as loud as he could on his armpit. His hand throbbed in pain, but he didn't stop.

'Follow the farts! Follow the farts!' he and Matthew called out.

One by one, the Penleydale Sea Squirts paddled and splashed, coughing and gasping, towards the sound of Danny's armpit. As each Squirt appeared, Matt helped them out, keeping a tally of the kids to make sure they were all there. The rescued children clambered out of the water and sat together against

the wall, licking the tasty mess off their hands and faces.

'Everyone's out,' said Matthew as he pulled the last Sea Squirt from the pool. 'Except . . .'

Natalie appeared in front of Danny, her hair plastered across her face like a horrible yellow mask. 'What have you done *this* time?' she growled.

Danny blew a particularly noisy armpit-trump at her. 'It wasn't me!' he protested.

The lemon fog was now so dense that Danny could see no more than an arm's length in front of him. The powder was choking and sweet. 'I'll go first,' he said to the kids. 'Stick close to each other, and remember, everyone: follow the farts!'

As the long line of children snaked out of the building with Danny leading the way, they began to sing 'Old MacDonald Had a Farm' to his armpit-music.

'Hey, Danny,' said Matthew. 'You're the Pied *Parper* of Penleydale.'

Outside the Sports Centre, fire engines, police cars and ambulances filled the road, their blue lights flashing urgently. People scurried here and there, calling frantic instructions to each other. Tempest Road was strewn with debris and broken biscuits from the Crumbly Crunch factory.

The Sea Squirts huddled together, shivering in the chilly air.

'Where's Trevor?' asked Matthew suddenly.

'He must still be in the pool!' said Danny.

He raced back into the Sports Centre. 'Trevor! Where are you?' he called into the murky yellow gloom.

'Help! I can't move! I'm trapped!' a voice spluttered.

'Don't worry,' shouted Danny. 'I'll rescue you.'

He
jumped
into the
water
at the
shallow

end and swam as hard
and as fast as he could.

He couldn't see The Line, but he knew when he had reached it because his heart began to drum a crazy rhythm and his tummy did a tingly dance to it.

Trevor shouted again. 'Hurry! Help me!'

Without another thought, Danny took a huge breath and swam across The Line. Moments later his hand touched the wall at the end of the pool and Trevor's face appeared right in front of him, covered in yellow slop, his mouth and nose just above the surface.

'I jumped in to rescue people,' he gasped. 'But my whistle's got tangled up in the filter and the string's twisted tight!'

Danny groped below the water, his hand searching The Grid's metal teeth. He felt clumps of hair and a soft square of sticking plaster, but then his fingers found something small and hard.

'Got it!' he cried.

But Trevor was still stuck.

In Danny's hand lay not a whistle, but a big, fat, dead cockroach, its brown, spiky legs pointing up at him.

'Ace!' he cried, dropping the insect back in the water and rummaging around again on the surface of the grill. Danny thought about the monster python lurking in the dark drain. *It's just a daft story*, he told himself.

At last Danny's fingers located the whistle and he began to twist and turn it, trying to wiggle it free. Suddenly it came loose and Trevor was able to raise his head above the water. Together they made their way to the metal ladders in the corner and climbed out.

'Thanks, kiddo,' gasped Trevor. 'I think your days in the shallow end are over. You've Crossed The Line and swum a length. *You* are in the Team!'

'Ace!' cried Danny.

As they emerged on to Tempest Road, Danny's mouth dropped open in amazement. Mingling amongst the firemen, police and paramedics were:

The Easter Bunny

A snowman

An astronaut

Father Christmas

A Tyrannosaurus rex

A bat

A penguin

A troupe of monkeys

King Henry VIII

and . . .

A bogey.

The T. rex bounded over.

'What's going on?' asked Danny.

'The "Fancy That!" costume shop over the road lent us these outfits so we wouldn't get cold,' explained the T. rex, in Matthew's voice.

At that moment, Mrs Bobbins, the shop manager, handed Danny a Superman suit. 'Put this on,' she said. 'It'll keep you warm.'

'Thanks,' said Danny. He pulled the costume on and the bright-red cape billowed out behind him.

'Guess which one's Natalie?' asked Matthew, waving one of his front claws at the other kids.

Danny smirked. 'Is she the bogey?'

'No,' answered Matthew. 'She's Nat the Bat!'

Danny Baker - Record Breaker

Dear Mr Bibby

I'm going to have Crumbly Crunch's new lemon-puff biscuits named after me, because I rescued the Penleydale Sea Squirts Swimming Club from the Lemon-puff Peril.

AND, I'm going to get two free packets a week forever!

Ace!

Each packet of Danny Baker Lemon Puffs will have seventeen biscuits in it. If I eat all thirty-four biscuits every week, how long will it take to break

my biscuit

Danny Baker Lemon Puffs

me

the world record for eating the most lemon
puffs?

Yours sincerely
Danny Baker

PS My mum and dad are really proud of me. Dad
says that he only ever saved goals, but I saved
people!

ARE YOU A RECORD
BREAKER ?

Dear Danny

Congratulations on your heroic rescue, which
I read about in the newspaper. I'm proud of
you too! You deserve the honour of having the
biscuits named after you. I love lemon puffs,
and often enjoy one with my afternoon cup of
tea.

The world record for Continuous Lemon Puff
Consumption is held by Lottie Gobbett, of Lower
Peover in Cheshire. She ate 558,451 biscuits
before realizing that she didn't actually
like lemon puffs. Unfortunately, by this time,
Lottie's nose had turned a strange canary-
yellow colour and glowed in the dark.

If you eat two packets a week (thirty-four

131

biscuits), you will be 325 years old by the time you break her record. And do you *really* want a yellow nose, Danny? What would Natalie say about *that*?

Now for the good news! I have checked all our records and I am thrilled to tell you that there has been no previous claim for the Armpit-fart-assisted Mass Rescue of People from Tornado-generated Lemon-puff Peril. Once again, you have *set* a new world record.

Well done! I am delighted to enclose your certificate for this wonderful and unique achievement.

Best wishes
Eric Bibby
Keeper of the Records

THE GREAT BIG BOOK
OF WORLD RECORDS

This is to certify that
Daniel 'Danny' Baker
set the world record for:
Armpit-fart-assisted Mass Rescue
of People (22)
from Tornado-generated Lemon-puff Peril

Keeper of the Records
Eric Bibby

World Record Breaker

The Gala was a great success. The Penleydale Sports
Centre gleamed after being scrubbed of all traces of
lemon-puff powder. Whistles blew, as families and
friends of the swimmers cheered from the packed

stand along one side of the pool.

Danny had worked hard practising his racing-dives. He glanced at his mum and dad as his relay race was about to start. Mum raised her arms and did a little clap, and Dad put his thumbs up. When Danny's turn came, he dived in, swam confidently up the pool and didn't even notice when he Crossed The Line. Even better, the team went on to win the race!

At the end, all the swimmers were presented with

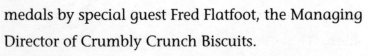

medals by special guest Fred Flatfoot, the Managing Director of Crumbly Crunch Biscuits.

'Ladies, gentlemen and children, we have one more *special* award to present today, to a very *special* boy,' he announced. 'Danny Baker, I am delighted to present you with the first packet of

Crumbly Crunch's new-and-improved recipe,
"Danny Baker Lemon Puffs", in honour of your
heroic actions on Lemon-puff-peril Day.'

Danny stepped forward, shook hands with Fred
Flatfoot, and took his tasty prize.

'Ace,' said
Danny.

'Cool,'
agreed
Matthew,
gazing at
the packet
of lemon-
puff biscuits.
Danny's
name was

emblazoned across it in letters two centimetres
high. 'That's better than having a stand named
after you, any day.'

'Yeah,' agreed Danny. 'You can't eat a stand!'

He held the packet proudly, high above his head.
The crowd rose to their feet to applaud their hero,

and the cheer that roared through the building
seemed as deafening to Danny as the booming of
the wild tornado.

'DA-NNY! DA-NNY! DA-NNY!'

Turn the page to read an exclusive extract of

THE WORLD'S
STICKIEST EARWAX

Out now!

The SweatSucker

BLADDERPOOL PLEASURE DOME

The SweatSucker challenge: we bet you'll sweat!

To the Keeper of the Records
The Great Big Book of World Records
London

Dear Mr Bibby

Last weekend, my swimming club, the Penleydale
Sea Squirts, had a day out at Bladderpool
Pleasure Dome. I took The SweatSucker
Challenge, and won! I rode this rollercoaster
that's so fast and scary, it makes you sweat
buckets! But when I went through the moisture-
meter at the end, I was as dry as a desert
in a dry spell. It hadn't sucked
MY sweat! I got free goes, and
stayed un-sweaty for twenty-five
rides before the Pleasure Dome
people made me stop. They gave
me a Certificate of Dryness
AND free admission to the park
for life! Ace!

Sweaty

moisture-
meter

dry

My best friend Matthew's sweat got really sucked. He was drenched. My sister, Natalie, and the other girls in the swimming club wouldn't go on it at all, because they don't think being sweaty is fun. Unluckily for them, when everyone's sweat got sucked on the fantastic reverse-triple-spiral-corkscrew-loop-the-loop, they were standing underneath and they got soaked!

sweat

I know I'm not the first to beat The SweatSucker, but has anyone else ever gone for twenty-five rides and stayed sweat-free?

Best wishes
Danny Baker

Dear Danny

The first person ever to beat The SweatSucker
also registered the Most Consecutive Rides
without Sweating. On 21 July 2007, Didier
Tremblay, of Quebec in Canada, managed to
complete 157 consecutive rides and not sweat
a single drop. However, nobody realized that
Didier had cheated! Before going on The
SweatSucker, he had covered his entire body
in Industrial Strength Antiperspirant. When
he took a shower and washed it off three
days later, all the pent-up sweat burst out
of every pore in his skin, as though he had
been punctured by millions of needles. Didier
collapsed dead in the bathtub, his shrivelled
body lying like a squeezed-out sponge in an
enormous pool of his own smelly sweat.

Since then, Bladderpool Pleasure Dome has limited successful riders to a maximum of twenty-five sweat-free goes. However, you are only the third person to have achieved this amazing feat! You are now twenty-five per cent of the way to completing the TerrorCoaster Grand Slam: taking on and beating the Top Four Rollercoaster Rides in the country (as voted for by the readers of *Cool Coasters Quarterly*).

The SweatSucker is in fourth place. The top three, in reverse order, are:

The brand-new BoneShaker at Tartan Towers Holiday Park, Saltimuchty, Scotland. It claims to shake your bones right out of your skin! So far, only two riders (0.00374%) have been able to stand up and walk the straight 10-m line at the end.

The BarfMaker at Ballynoggin's Leprechaun Leap Fun Centre, Northern Ireland. Drink your

'Compulsory Super-thick Banana Milkshake'
before you ride, and then try NOT to barf! This
rollercoaster is so whirly and swirly that so
far nobody (0.00000%) has been able to keep
their milkshake down!

And finally, the Most Awesome Rollercoaster in
Great Britain: The Pontypyddl PantWetter at Red
Dragonland in Wales, a ride so *seriously scary*,
it's *guaranteed* to make you wet your pants!

You could become the first person *ever* to ride
all four rollercoasters and not sweat, wobble,
vomit or wee! Go for it, Danny!

Best wishes
Eric Bibby
Keeper of the Records

Danny, Natalie, Mum and Dad drove home after spending a day out in the village of Pugswallop, at the 46th Annual World Rice-pudding-wrestling Championships.

'What a waste of a Sunday!' moaned Natalie.

'Be fair, Nat,' said Danny. 'I spent all last Sunday watching you swim up and down a pool in the County Swimming Trials. The least you can do is spend an afternoon watching me wrestle in rice pudding!'

'You didn't even win!'

'It was my first try!' protested Danny. 'The lad who beat me pudding-wrestles for Wales!'

His sister sniffed. 'At least you smell a bit sweeter than you normally do!'

Mum turned on the radio. The sound of Natalie's favourite boy band filled the car.

'Fab!' cried Natalie, and began to sing. *'Yoooooou are my one and only girrrrrl. Ooooooooooo, bay-bee.'*

'I can burp this song,' announced Danny, joining in with loud, ringing belches.

Natalie pulled a face. 'You're such a *child*!' she

sneered, sticking her fingers in her ears.

Soon they arrived in Penleydale. Dad turned on to the road over Hangman's Hump and they began to descend into Burly Bottoms.

'Mum! Tell him!' said Natalie. 'Danny's reading a book!'

'Excellent!' replied Mum.

'He's only trying to make himself carsick so he can break some disgusting record, like . . . Completely Filling a Car with Vomit!'

'Ace idea, Nat!' laughed Danny. 'I wonder what the record is.'

'Stop bickering, you two!' ordered Mum. 'If you keep this up over the half-term holiday, you'll drive

me mad! The doctor said I have to rest now that the baby's nearly here.'

'I'll go mad with boredom,' said Natalie. 'Kaylie and Kylie are going to Tenerife next week. What am *I* going to do?'

'You can play footy with me and Matt,' suggested Danny.

'As if!'

Walking through their front door, they heard the telephone ring and Dad hurried into the kitchen to answer it.

Mum, Danny and Natalie went into the living room. The floor was strewn with old baby things: plastic toys and tiny clothes, a pushchair, a potty and a dismantled cot.

Mum sat down, rummaged through a box and held up two little mittens, one pink and one blue.

'I wonder which of these I'll be using for the new baby,' she said.

'Pink,' said Natalie. 'It's *totally* going to be a girl.'

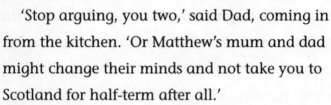

'Blue,' said Danny. 'It's *got* to be a boy.'

'Stop arguing, you two,' said Dad, coming in from the kitchen. 'Or Matthew's mum and dad might change their minds and not take you to Scotland for half-term after all.'

'What?!' cried the children.

'The rollercoaster at Tartan Towers has gone on the blink,' he explained. 'Matthew's dad's going up to Scotland on Saturday to fix it. They thought they'd give your mum a break over the holidays and take you two with them.'

'Ace!' exclaimed Danny. 'Mr Bibby says The BoneShaker's the third best ride in Britain! It must be *really* brilliant if it beats The SweatSucker.'

Natalie gave a small growl. 'So I have to spend

all next week
with him and
Matthew?'

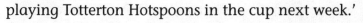

'Are you coming,
Dad?' asked Danny.

'No, I can't get
away from work,'
Dad replied. 'We're
playing Totterton Hotspoons in the cup next week.'

'That's settled then,' said Mum. 'You'd both
better start packing.'

THE WORLD'S BIGGEST BOGEY

STEVE HARTLEY

TO THE MANAGER
The Great Big Book
of World Records
London

Dear Sir,
I have been collecting
bogeys from my nose for the
last two years.
I have stuck them all together
to make one enormous bogey. It
measures 5.3 cm in diameter and
weighs 3.6 grams. Is this a record?

Yours faithfully,

Danny Baker

(Aged nine and a bit)

Join Danny as he attempts to smash a
load of revolting records, including:

LOUDEST TRUMP!
CHEESIEST FEET!
NITTIEST SCALP!

OUT NOW!

A selected list of titles available from Macmillan Children's Books

The prices shown below are correct at the time of going to press. However, Macmillan Publishers reserves the right to show new retail prices on covers, which may differ from those previously advertised.

Steve Hartley

Danny Baker Record Breaker:

The World's Biggest Bogey	978-0-330-50916-9	£4.99
The World's Awesomest Air-Barf	978-0-330-50917-6	£4.99
The World's Stickiest Earwax	978-0-330-50919-0	£4.99

Andy Griffiths & Terry Denton

Help! My Parents Think I'm a Robot (and 9 other Just Shocking! Stories)	978-0-330-45426-1	£4.99
Help! I'm Being Chased by a Giant Slug (and 8 other Just Disgusting! stories)	978-0-330-50411-9	£4.99
Help! I'm Trapped In My Best Friend's Nose (and 8 other Just Crazy! stories)	978-0-330-50410-2	£4.99
What Bumosaur Is That?	978-0-330-44752-2	£4.99

All Pan Macmillan titles can be ordered from our website, www.panmacmillan.com, or from your local bookshop and are also available by post from:

Bookpost, PO Box 29, Douglas, Isle of Man IM99 1BQ

Credit cards accepted. For details:
Telephone: 01624 677237
Fax: 01624 670923
Email: bookshop@enterprise.net
www.bookpost.co.uk

Free postage and packing in the United Kingdom